D1399101

Billy Batson and the Magic of Shazam!

STONE ARCH BOOKS
a capstone imprint

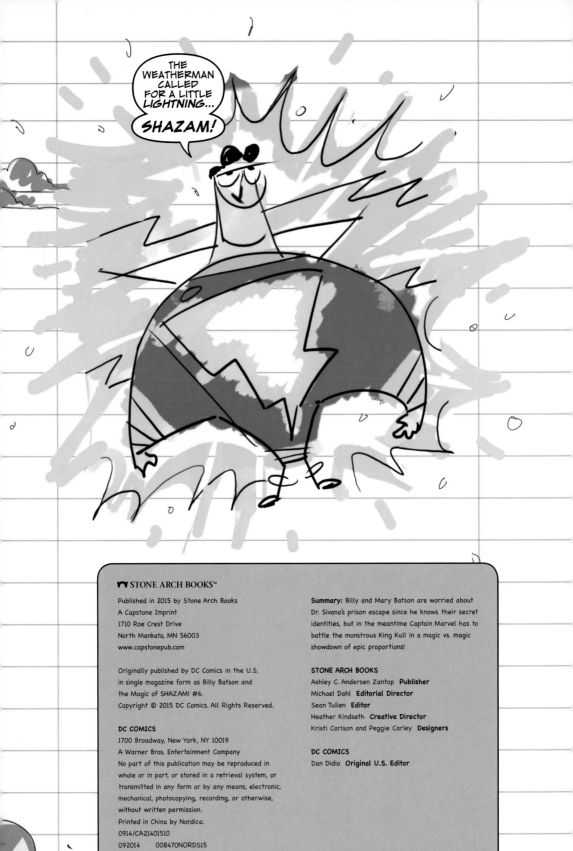

▼▼ STONE ARCH BOOKS™

Published in 2015 by Stone Arch Books
A Capstone Imprint
1710 Roe Crest Drive
North Mankato, MN 56003
www.capstonepub.com

Originally published by DC Comics in the U.S.
in single magazine form as Billy Batson and
the Magic of SHAZAM! #6.
Copyright © 2015 DC Comics. All Rights Reserved.

DC COMICS
1700 Broadway, New York, NY 10019
A Warner Bros. Entertainment Company

Printed in China by Nordica.
0914/CA21401510
092014   008470NORDS15

Cataloging-in-Publication Data is available at the Library
of Congress website.
ISBN: 978-1-4342-9657-3 (library binding)

Summary: Billy and Mary Batson are worried about
Dr. Sivana's prison escape since he knows their secret
identities, but in the meantime Captain Marvel has to
battle the monstrous King Kull in a magic vs. magic
showdown of epic proportions!

STONE ARCH BOOKS
Ashley C. Andersen Zantop **Publisher**
Michael Dahl **Editorial Director**
Sean Tulien **Editor**
Heather Kindseth **Creative Director**
Kristi Carlson and Peggie Carley **Designers**

DC COMICS
Dan Didio **Original U.S. Editor**

BILLY BATSON AND THE MAGIC OF SHAZAM!

To Be King!

Art Baltazar & Franco .... writers
Stephen DeStefano .... illustrator
Dave Tanguay .... colorist

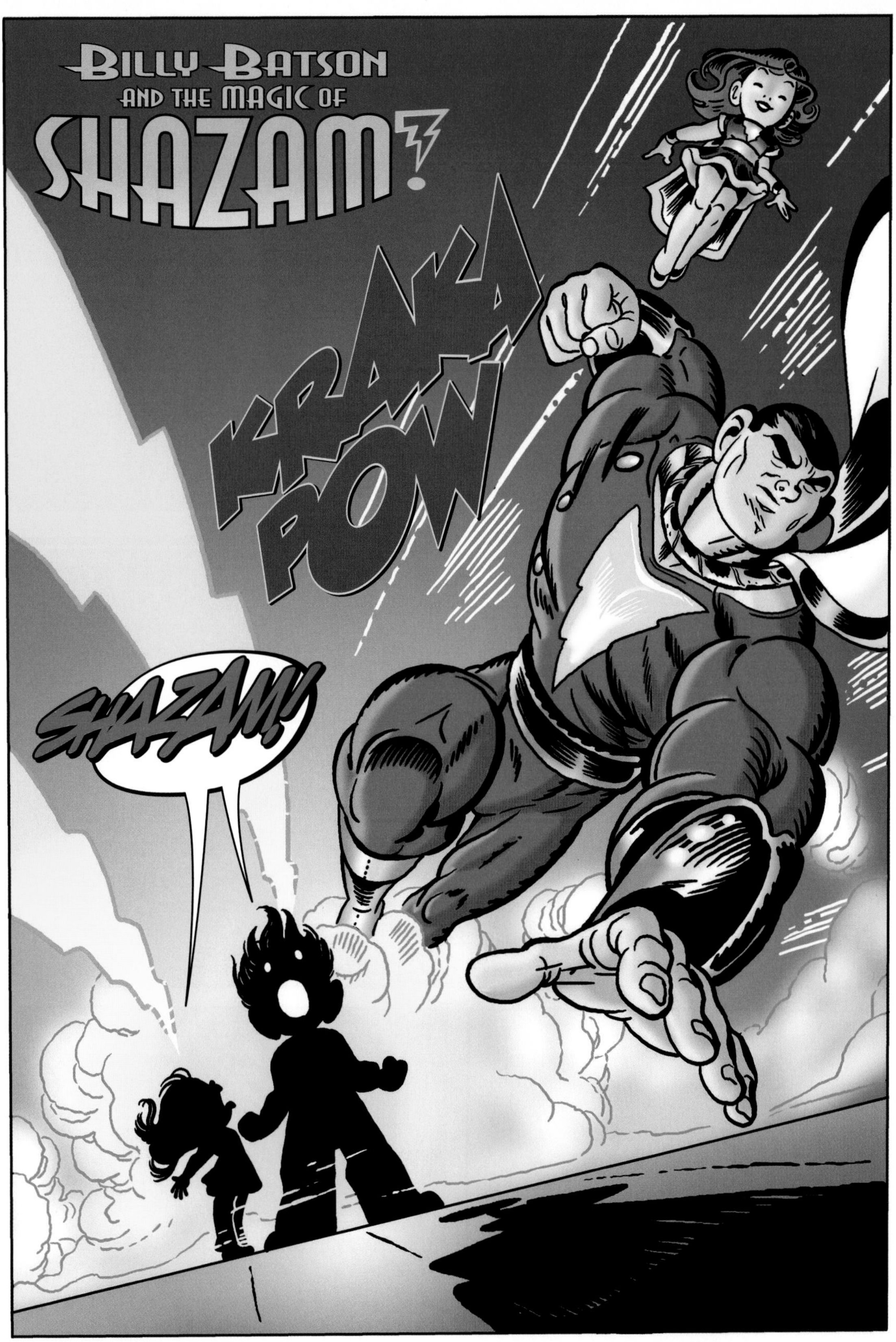
BILLY BATSON AND THE MAGIC OF SHAZAM!
KRAKA POW
SHAZAM!

to be KING

Written By: Art Baltazar & Franco
Art By: Stephen DeStefano
Colors: David Tanguay
Cover: J. Bone
Asst. Editor: Simona Martore
Editors: Dan Didio & Rachel Gluckstern

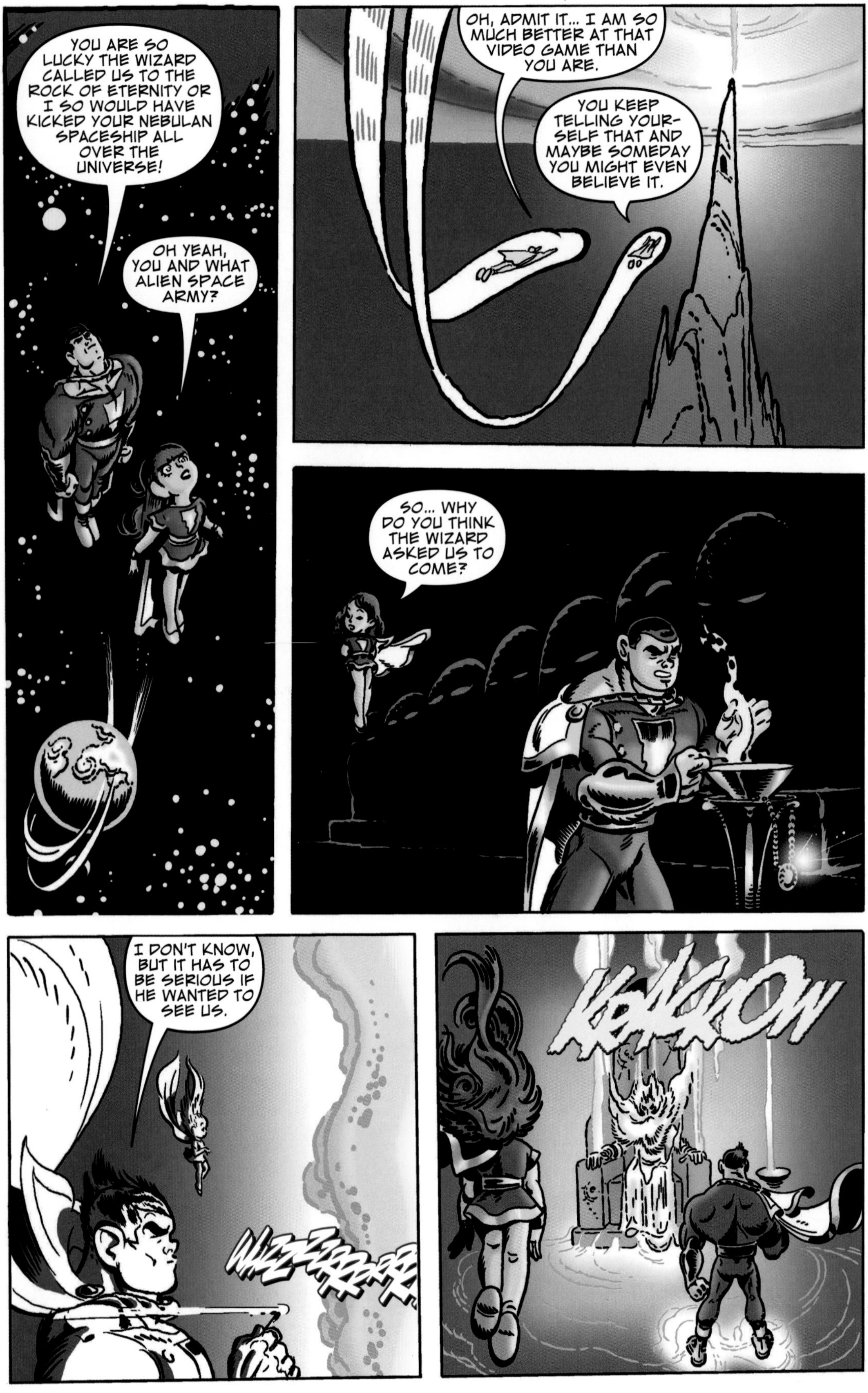

YOU ARE SO LUCKY THE WIZARD CALLED US TO THE ROCK OF ETERNITY OR I SO WOULD HAVE KICKED YOUR NEBULAN SPACESHIP ALL OVER THE UNIVERSE!
OH YEAH, YOU AND WHAT ALIEN SPACE ARMY?
OH, ADMIT IT... I AM SO MUCH BETTER AT THAT VIDEO GAME THAN YOU ARE.
YOU KEEP TELLING YOURSELF THAT AND MAYBE SOMEDAY YOU MIGHT EVEN BELIEVE IT.
SO... WHY DO YOU THINK THE WIZARD ASKED US TO COME?
I DON'T KNOW, BUT IT HAS TO BE SERIOUS IF HE WANTED TO SEE US.
WHZZZRRRRR
KRAKOW

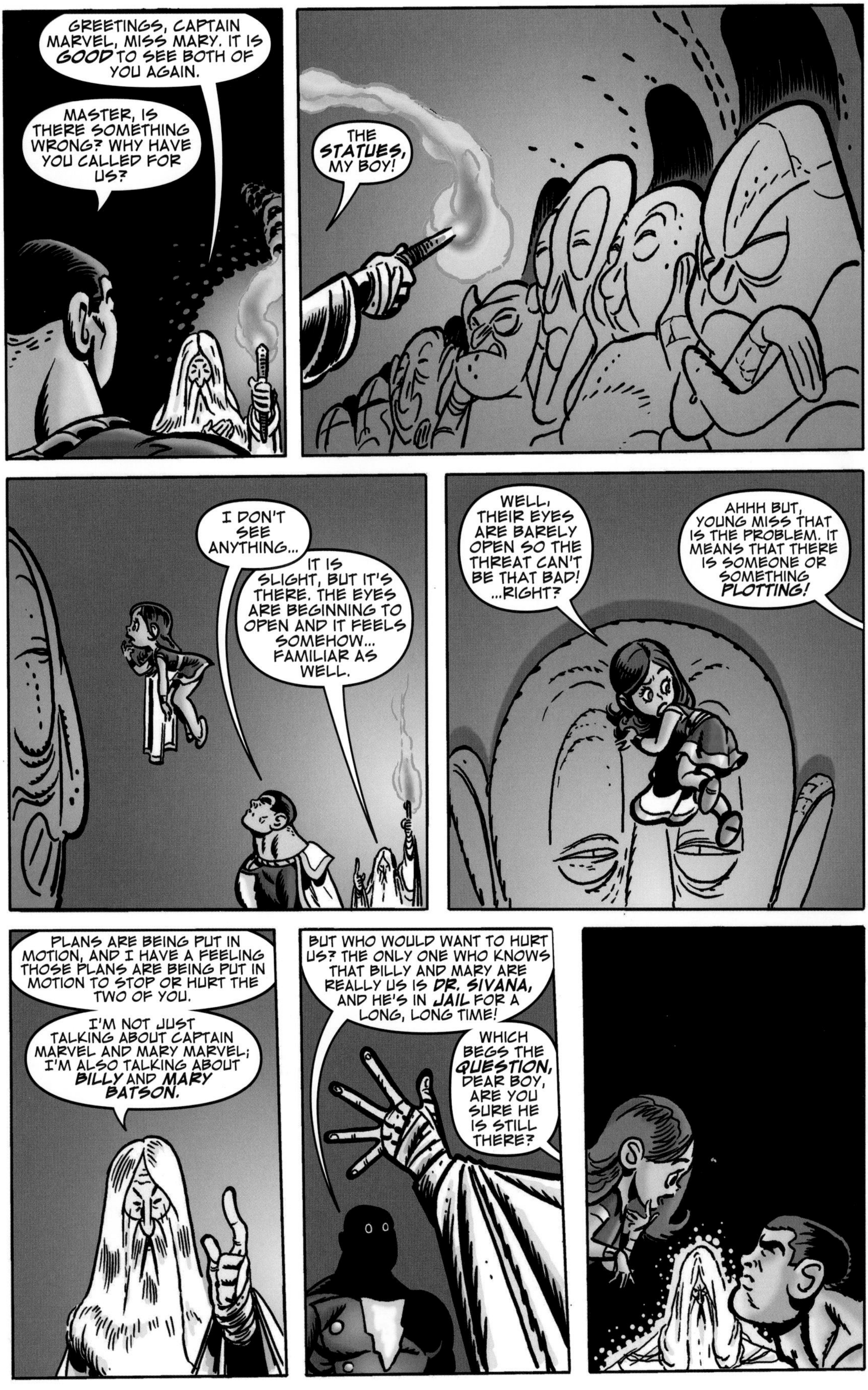
GREETINGS, CAPTAIN MARVEL, MISS MARY. IT IS GOOD TO SEE BOTH OF YOU AGAIN.
MASTER, IS THERE SOMETHING WRONG? WHY HAVE YOU CALLED FOR US?
THE STATUES, MY BOY!
I DON'T SEE ANYTHING...
IT IS SLIGHT, BUT IT'S THERE. THE EYES ARE BEGINNING TO OPEN AND IT FEELS SOMEHOW... FAMILIAR AS WELL.
WELL, THEIR EYES ARE BARELY OPEN SO THE THREAT CAN'T BE THAT BAD! ...RIGHT?
AHHH BUT, YOUNG MISS THAT IS THE PROBLEM. IT MEANS THAT THERE IS SOMEONE OR SOMETHING PLOTTING!
PLANS ARE BEING PUT IN MOTION, AND I HAVE A FEELING THOSE PLANS ARE BEING PUT IN MOTION TO STOP OR HURT THE TWO OF YOU.
I'M NOT JUST TALKING ABOUT CAPTAIN MARVEL AND MARY MARVEL; I'M ALSO TALKING ABOUT BILLY AND MARY BATSON.
BUT WHO WOULD WANT TO HURT US? THE ONLY ONE WHO KNOWS THAT BILLY AND MARY ARE REALLY US IS DR. SIVANA, AND HE'S IN JAIL FOR A LONG, LONG TIME!
WHICH BEGS THE QUESTION, DEAR BOY, ARE YOU SURE HE IS STILL THERE?

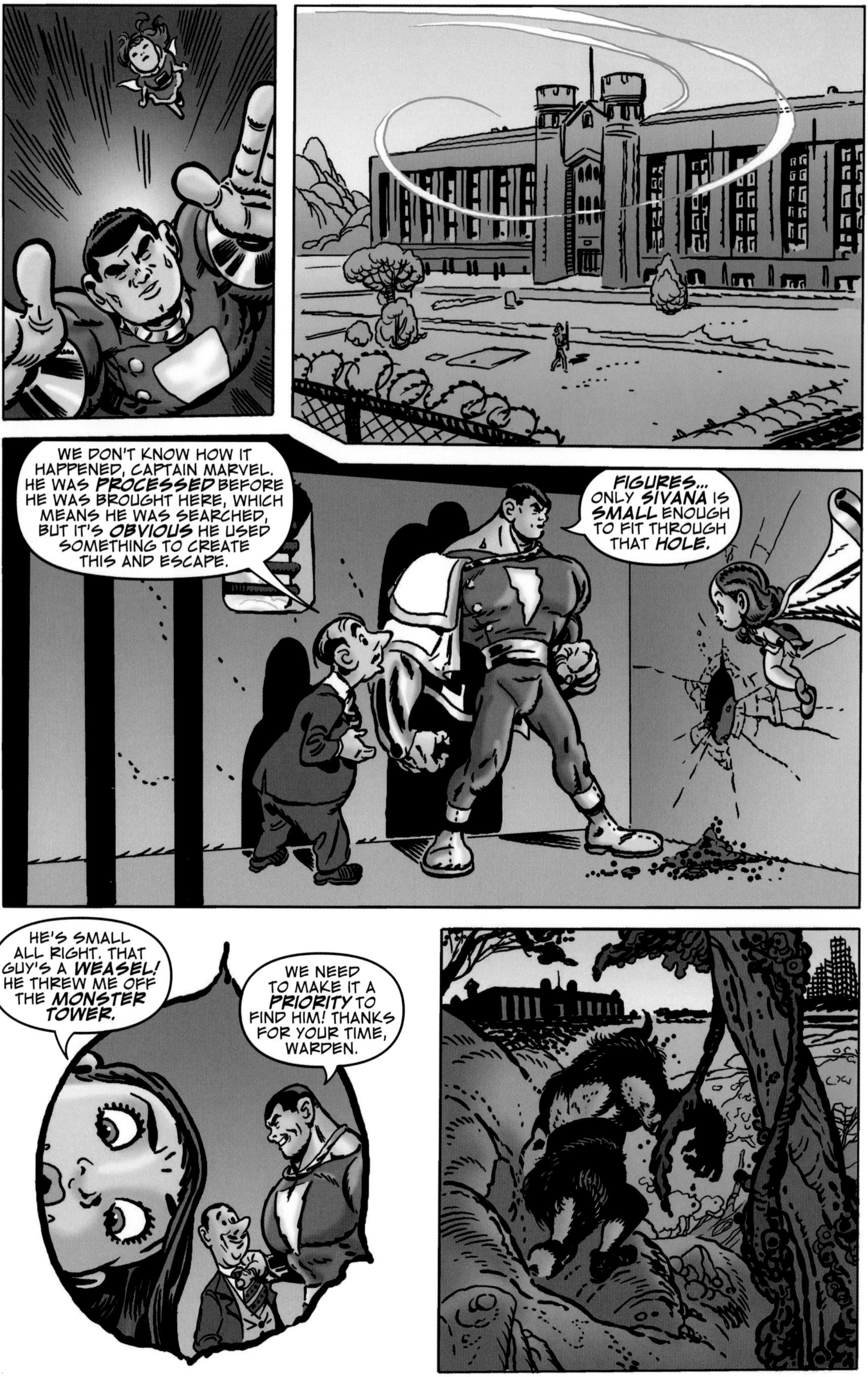
WE DON'T KNOW HOW IT HAPPENED, CAPTAIN MARVEL. HE WAS PROCESSED BEFORE HE WAS BROUGHT HERE, WHICH MEANS HE WAS SEARCHED, BUT IT'S OBVIOUS HE USED SOMETHING TO CREATE THIS AND ESCAPE.
FIGURES... ONLY SIVANA IS SMALL ENOUGH TO FIT THROUGH THAT HOLE.
HE'S SMALL ALL RIGHT. THAT GUY'S A WEASEL! HE THREW ME OFF THE MONSTER TOWER.
WE NEED TO MAKE IT A PRIORITY TO FIND HIM! THANKS FOR YOUR TIME, WARDEN.

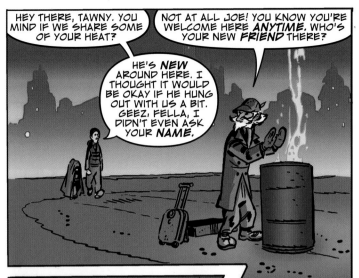

HEY THERE, TAWNY. YOU MIND IF WE SHARE SOME OF YOUR HEAT?

NOT AT ALL JOE! YOU KNOW YOU'RE WELCOME HERE *ANYTIME.* WHO'S YOUR NEW *FRIEND* THERE?

HE'S *NEW* AROUND HERE. I THOUGHT IT WOULD BE OKAY IF HE HUNG OUT WITH US A BIT. GEEZ, FELLA, I DIDN'T EVEN ASK YOUR *NAME.*

JUST CALL ME *'DOC,'* FRIEND.

NICE TO MEET YOU, DOC.

SNAP CRACK

WHAT? WHAT IS *THAT?*

KIDS! RUN!!

9

THIS IS **SERIOUS**, MARY...

WHIZ

I'M WORRIED BECAUSE SIVANA KNOWS OUR...

...SECRET IDENTITIES! WE NEED TO FIGURE OUT **WHERE** HE IS!

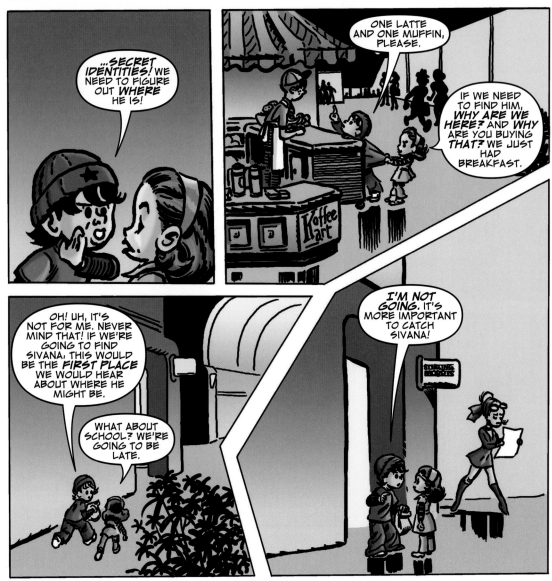

ONE LATTE AND ONE MUFFIN, PLEASE.

IF WE NEED TO FIND HIM, **WHY ARE WE HERE?** AND **WHY** ARE YOU BUYING **THAT?** WE JUST HAD BREAKFAST.

OH! UH, IT'S NOT FOR ME. NEVER MIND THAT! IF WE'RE GOING TO FIND SIVANA, THIS WOULD BE THE **FIRST PLACE** WE WOULD HEAR ABOUT WHERE HE MIGHT BE.

WHAT ABOUT SCHOOL? WE'RE GOING TO BE LATE.

I'M **NOT GOING.** IT'S MORE IMPORTANT TO CATCH SIVANA!

GOOD MORNING, MS. FIDELITY!

OH! HEY, THANKS, SHORT STUFF!

HEY, YOU *TWO!!* SIVANA HAS ESCAPED FROM PRISON!! IT CAME OVER THE WIRE LAST NIGHT. GET OUT TO THE PENITENTIARY AND SEE WHAT YOU CAN FIND OUT.

RIGHT, CHIEF!

STERLING MORRIS

BUT, BILLY... WHAT ABOUT *SCHOOL?*

I'M GOING TO RIDE AROUND WITH HELEN TO SEE WHAT WE CAN FIND. YOU GO AHEAD.

YOU SHOULDN'T DITCH SCHOOL! THE ONLY REASON YOU'RE NOT GOING IS BECAUSE YOU LIKE HELEN AND JUST WANT TO HANG OUT WITH HER.

WHAT? I DO NOT!

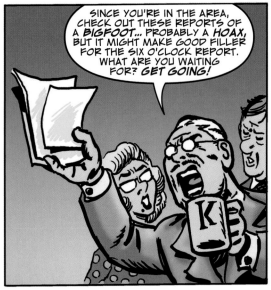

SINCE YOU'RE IN THE AREA, CHECK OUT THESE REPORTS OF A *BIGFOOT*... PROBABLY A *HOAX*, BUT IT MIGHT MAKE GOOD FILLER FOR THE SIX O'CLOCK REPORT. WHAT ARE YOU WAITING FOR? *GET GOING!*

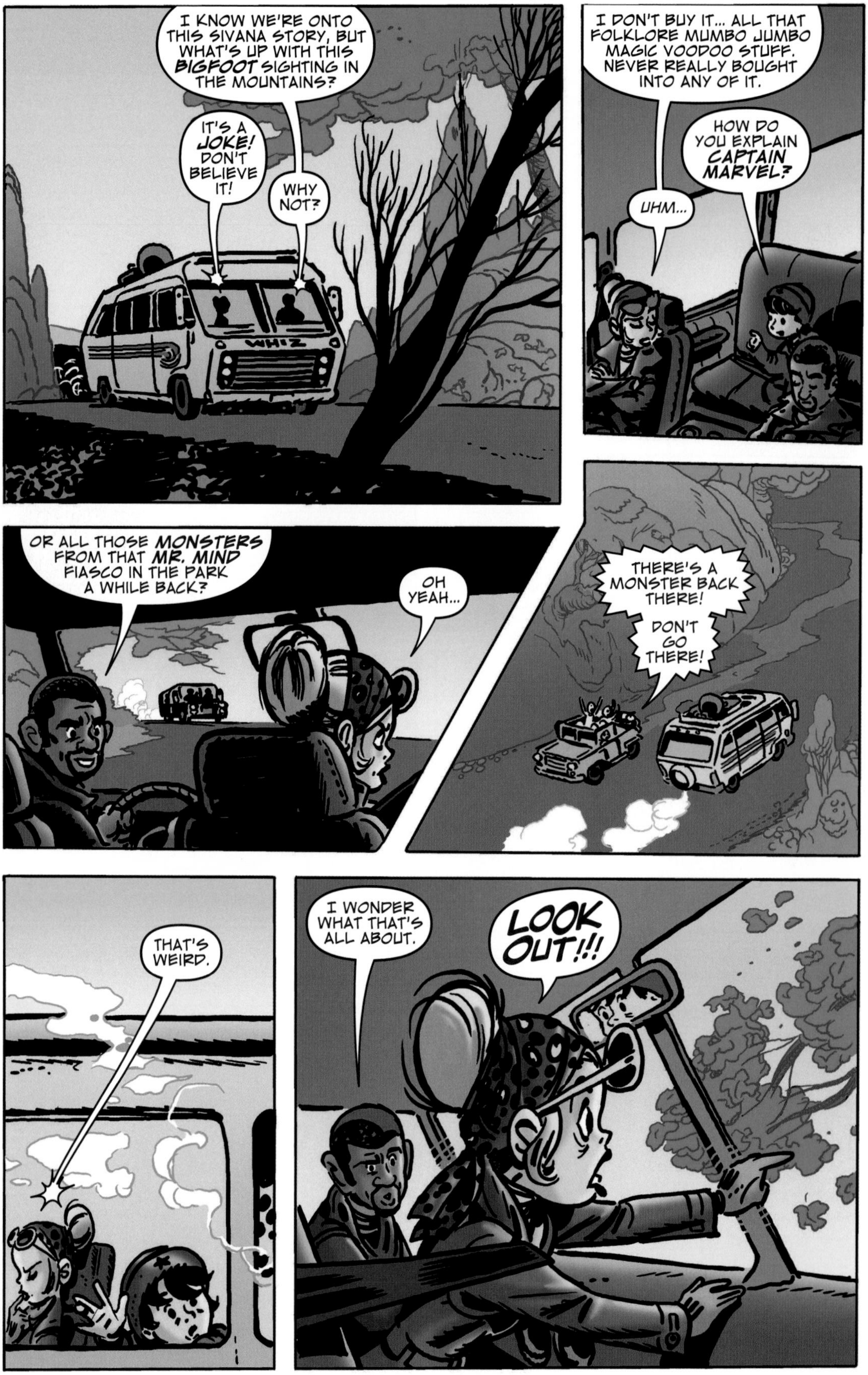
I KNOW WE'RE ONTO THIS SIVANA STORY, BUT WHAT'S UP WITH THIS BIGFOOT SIGHTING IN THE MOUNTAINS?
IT'S A JOKE! DON'T BELIEVE IT!
WHY NOT?
WHIZ
I DON'T BUY IT... ALL THAT FOLKLORE MUMBO JUMBO MAGIC VOODOO STUFF. NEVER REALLY BOUGHT INTO ANY OF IT.
HOW DO YOU EXPLAIN CAPTAIN MARVEL?
UHM...
OR ALL THOSE MONSTERS FROM THAT MR. MIND FIASCO IN THE PARK A WHILE BACK?
OH YEAH...
THERE'S A MONSTER BACK THERE!
DON'T GO THERE!
THAT'S WEIRD.
I WONDER WHAT THAT'S ALL ABOUT.
LOOK OUT!!!

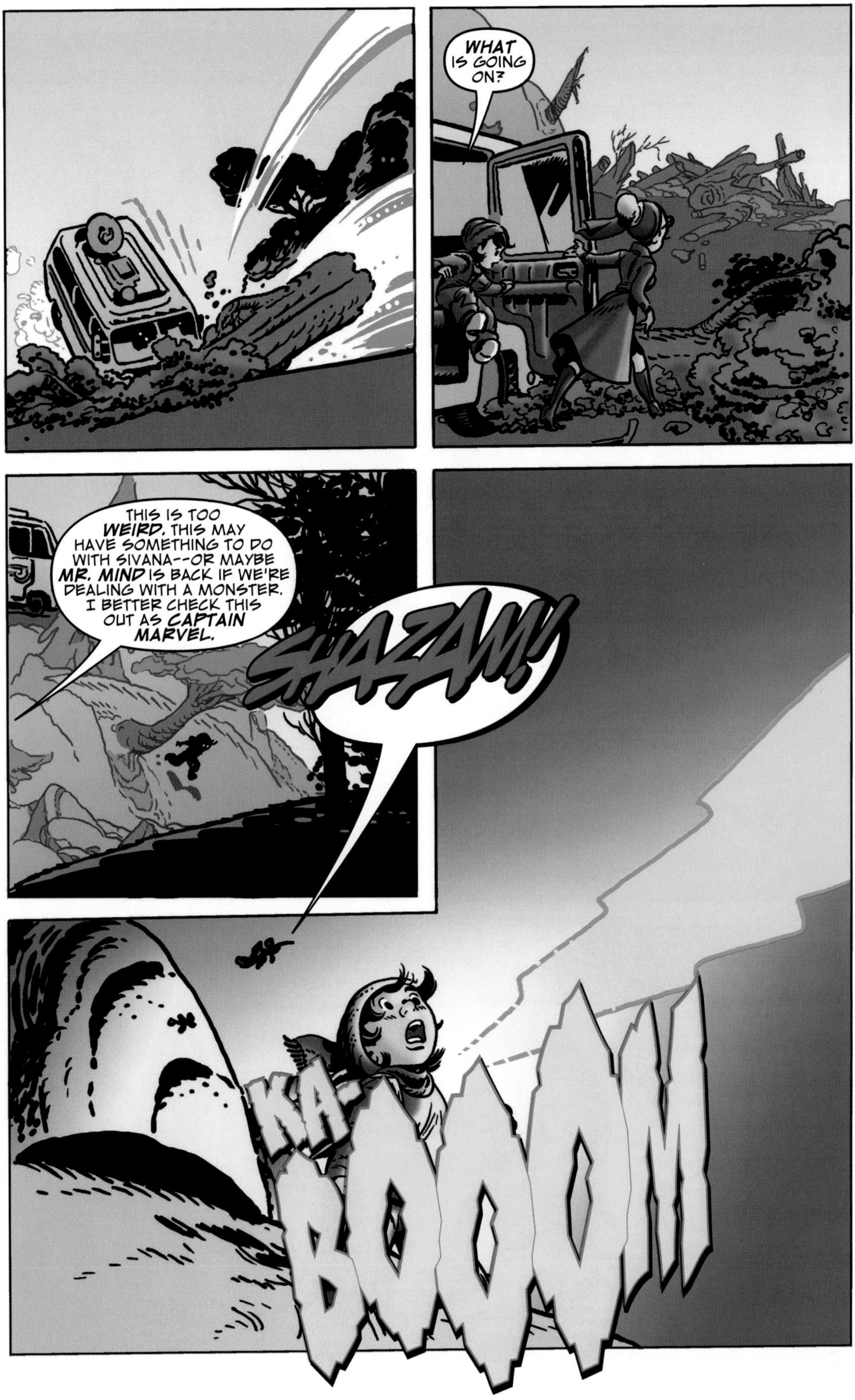
WHAT IS GOING ON?
THIS IS TOO WEIRD. THIS MAY HAVE SOMETHING TO DO WITH SIVANA--OR MAYBE MR. MIND IS BACK IF WE'RE DEALING WITH A MONSTER. I BETTER CHECK THIS OUT AS CAPTAIN MARVEL.
SHAZAM!
KA-BOOOM

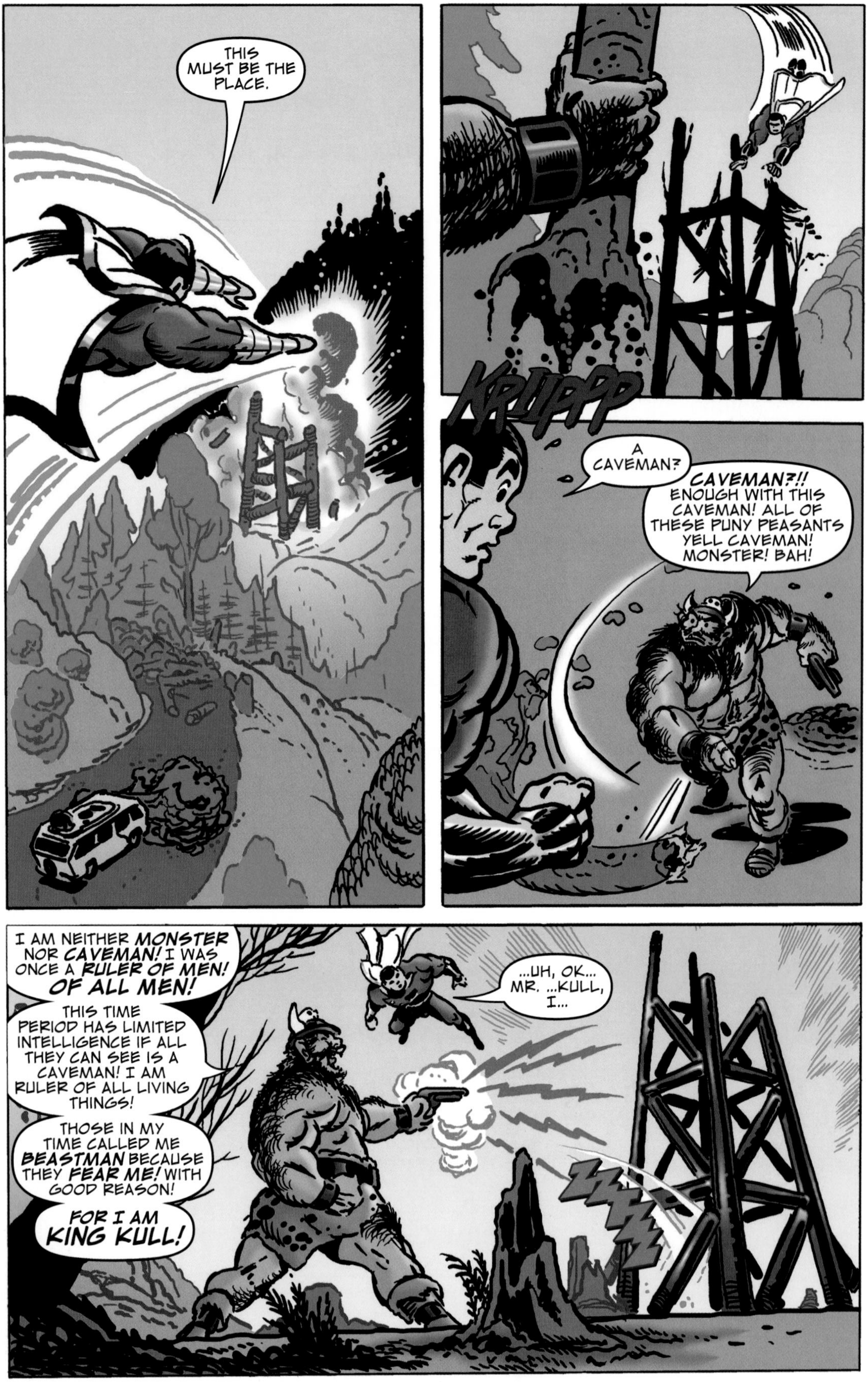
THIS MUST BE THE PLACE.
KRUPPP
A CAVEMAN?
CAVEMAN?!! ENOUGH WITH THIS CAVEMAN! ALL OF THESE PUNY PEASANTS YELL CAVEMAN! MONSTER! BAH!
I AM NEITHER MONSTER NOR CAVEMAN! I WAS ONCE A RULER OF MEN! OF ALL MEN!
THIS TIME PERIOD HAS LIMITED INTELLIGENCE IF ALL THEY CAN SEE IS A CAVEMAN! I AM RULER OF ALL LIVING THINGS!
THOSE IN MY TIME CALLED ME BEASTMAN BECAUSE THEY FEAR ME! WITH GOOD REASON!
FOR I AM KING KULL!
...UH, OK... MR. ...KULL, I...
ZZZZ

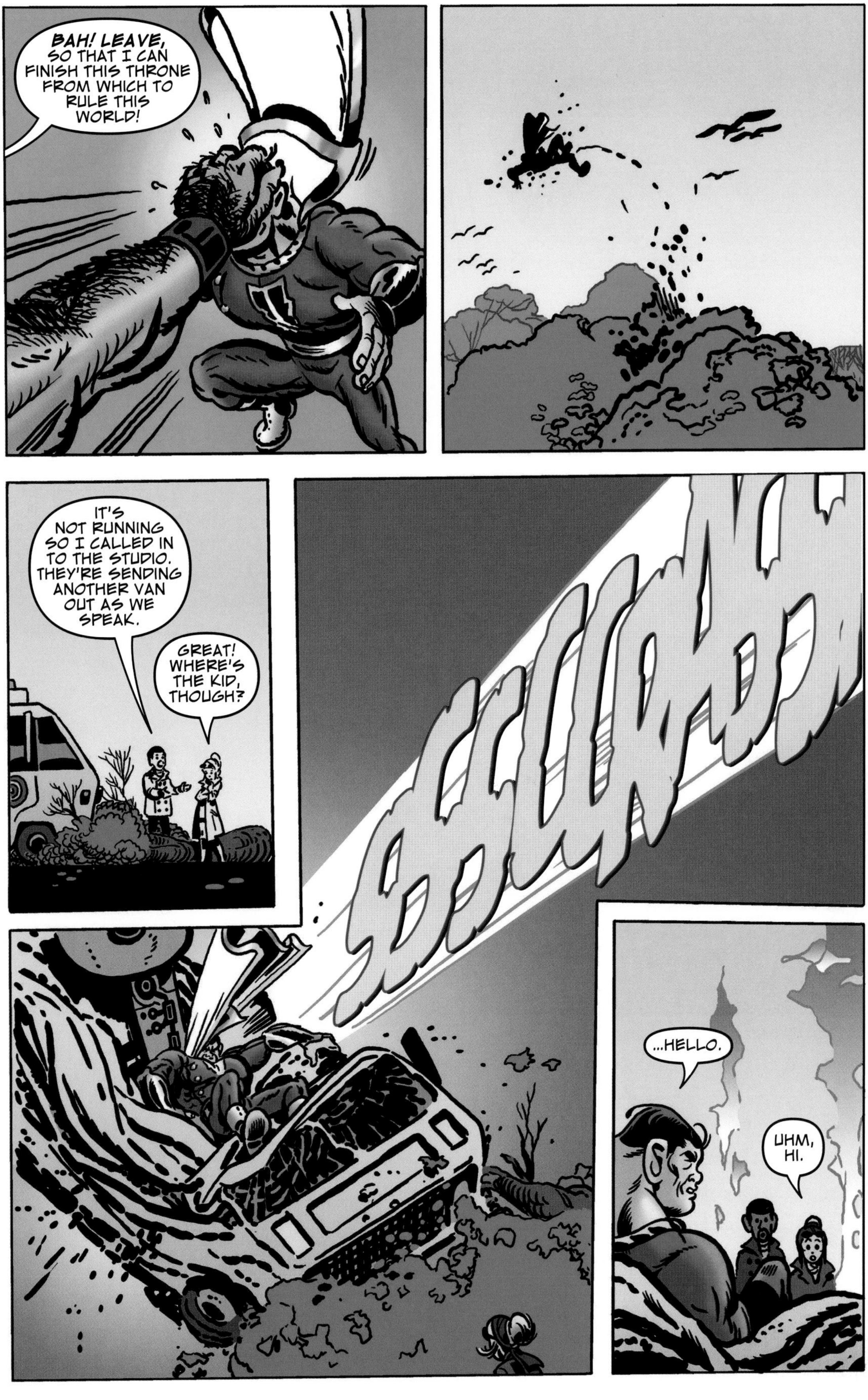
BAH! LEAVE, SO THAT I CAN FINISH THIS THRONE FROM WHICH TO RULE THIS WORLD!
IT'S NOT RUNNING SO I CALLED IN TO THE STUDIO. THEY'RE SENDING ANOTHER VAN OUT AS WE SPEAK.
GREAT! WHERE'S THE KID, THOUGH?
...HELLO.
UHM, HI.

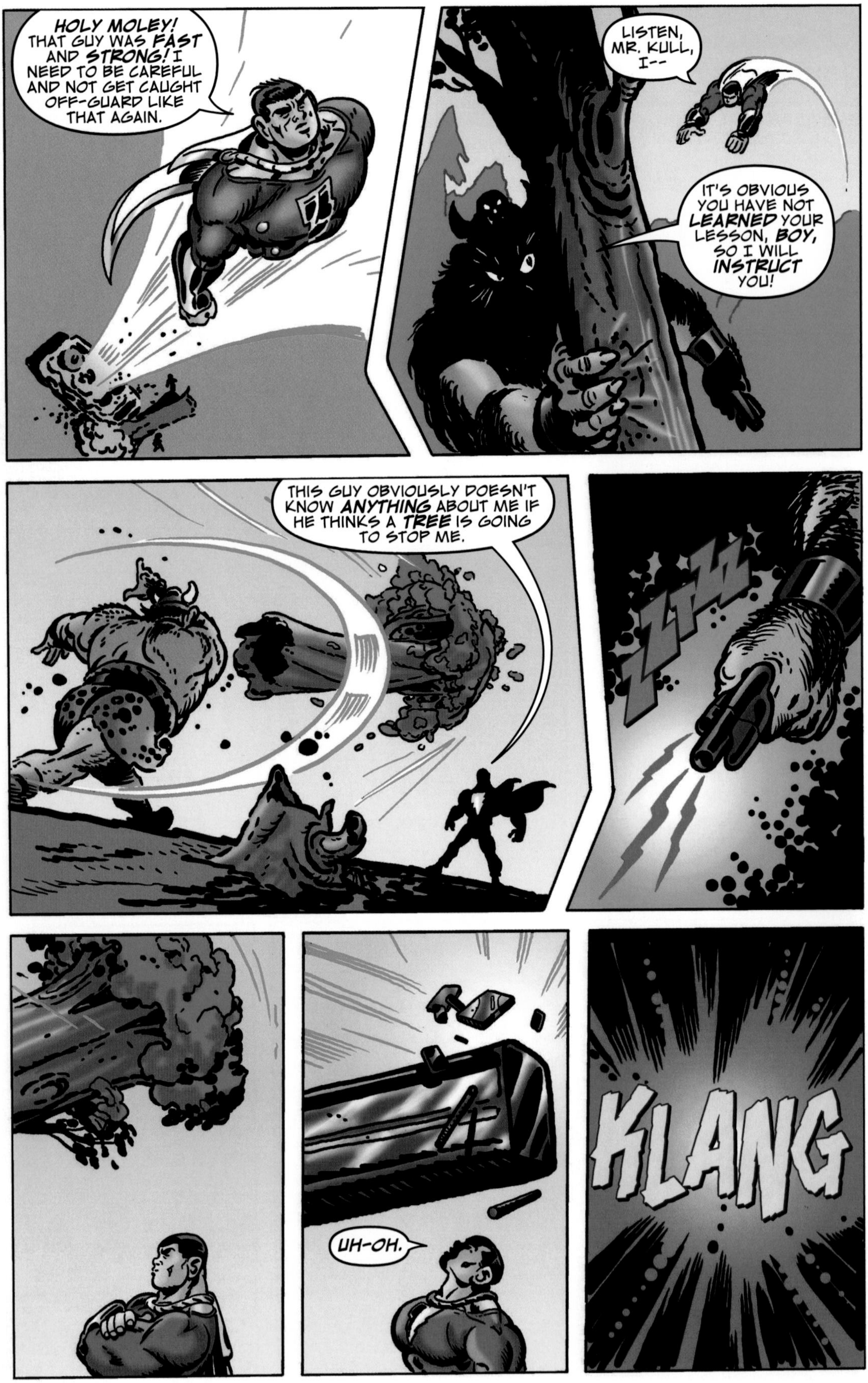
HOLY MOLEY! THAT GUY WAS FAST AND STRONG! I NEED TO BE CAREFUL AND NOT GET CAUGHT OFF-GUARD LIKE THAT AGAIN.
LISTEN, MR. KULL, I--
IT'S OBVIOUS YOU HAVE NOT LEARNED YOUR LESSON, BOY, SO I WILL INSTRUCT YOU!
THIS GUY OBVIOUSLY DOESN'T KNOW ANYTHING ABOUT ME IF HE THINKS A TREE IS GOING TO STOP ME.
ZZZZ
UH-OH.
KLANG

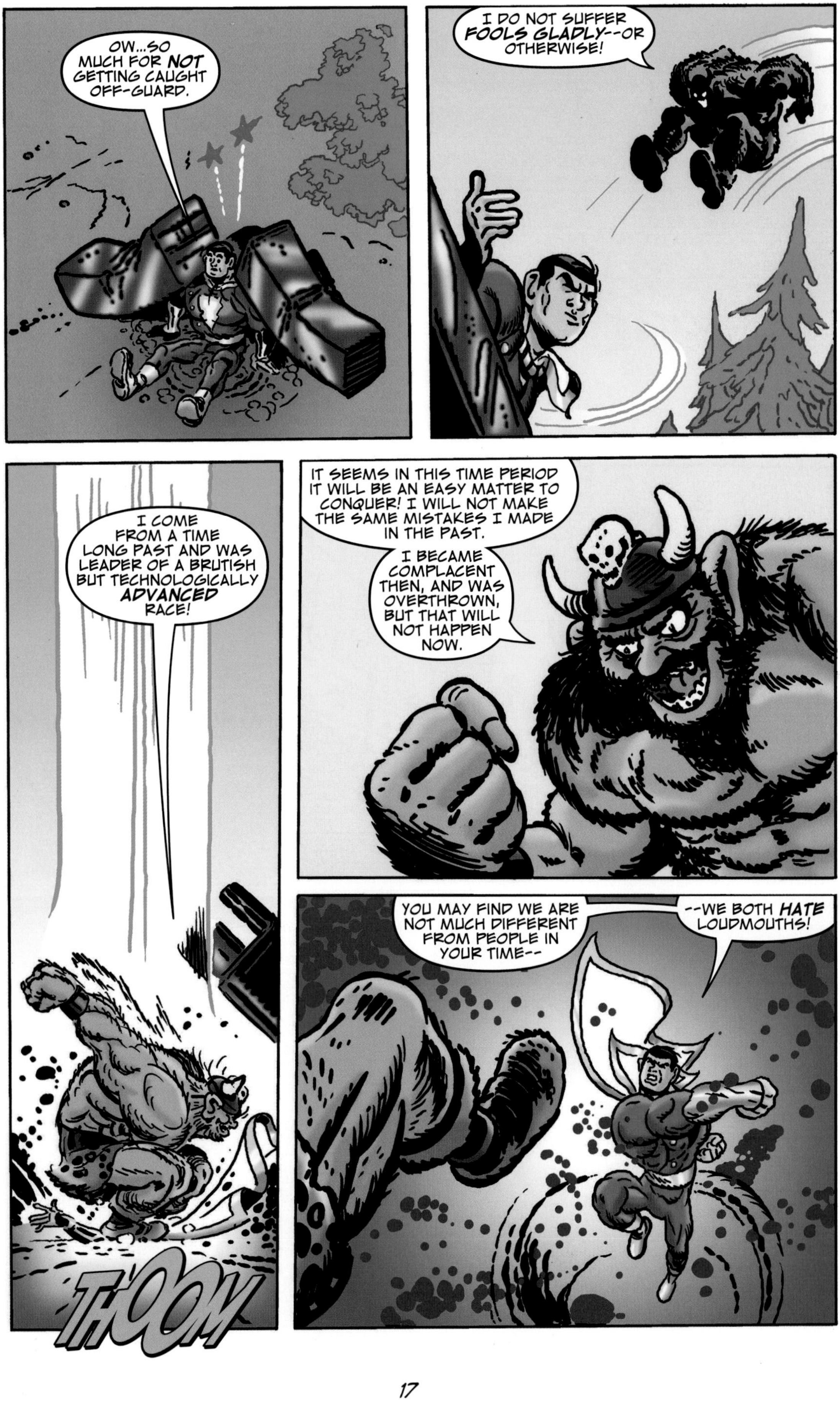
OW...SO MUCH FOR NOT GETTING CAUGHT OFF-GUARD.
I DO NOT SUFFER FOOLS GLADLY--OR OTHERWISE!
I COME FROM A TIME LONG PAST AND WAS LEADER OF A BRUTISH BUT TECHNOLOGICALLY ADVANCED RACE!
THOOM
IT SEEMS IN THIS TIME PERIOD IT WILL BE AN EASY MATTER TO CONQUER! I WILL NOT MAKE THE SAME MISTAKES I MADE IN THE PAST.
I BECAME COMPLACENT THEN, AND WAS OVERTHROWN, BUT THAT WILL NOT HAPPEN NOW.
YOU MAY FIND WE ARE NOT MUCH DIFFERENT FROM PEOPLE IN YOUR TIME--
--WE BOTH HATE LOUDMOUTHS!

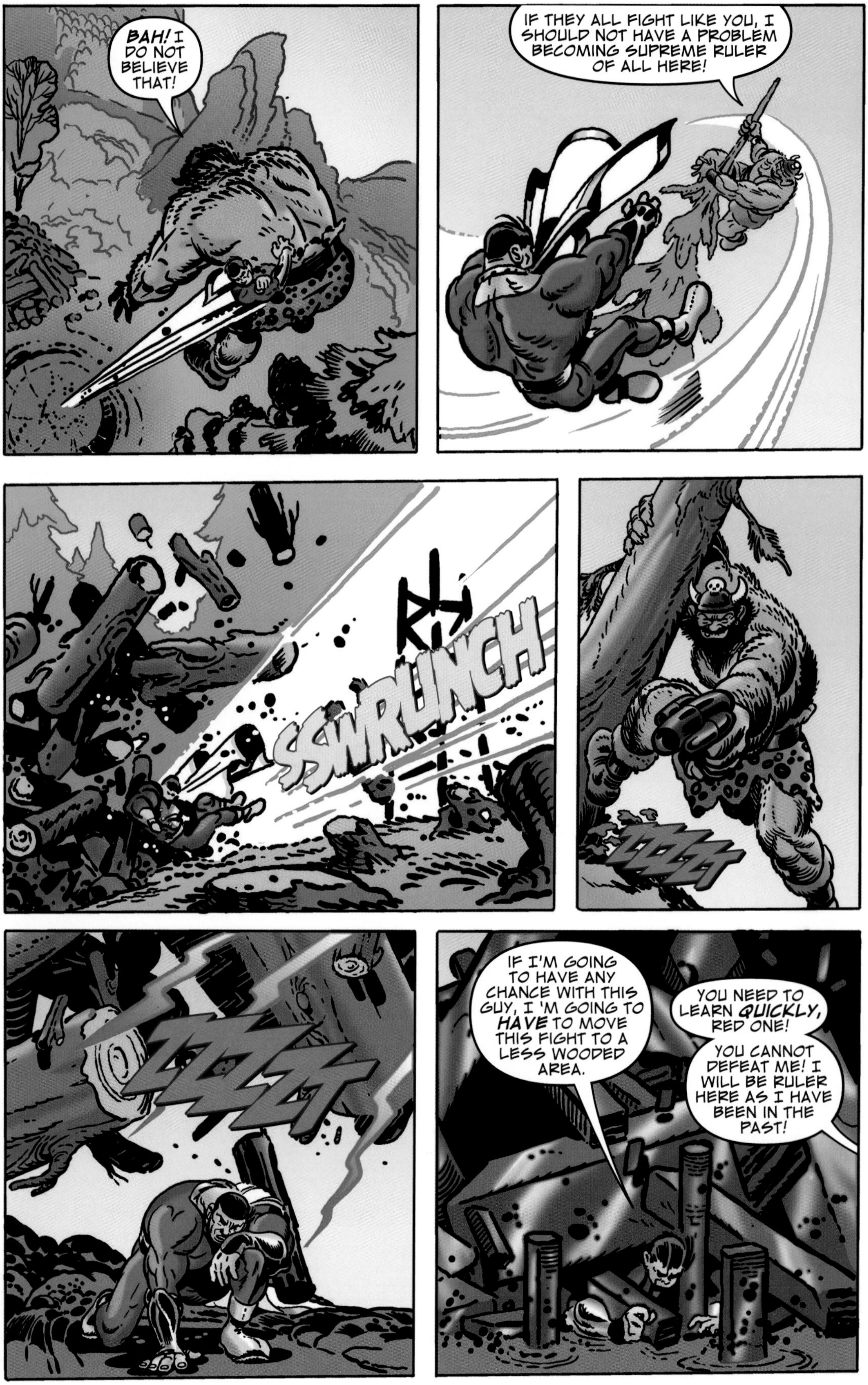
BAH! I DO NOT BELIEVE THAT!
IF THEY ALL FIGHT LIKE YOU, I SHOULD NOT HAVE A PROBLEM BECOMING SUPREME RULER OF ALL HERE!
SSWRUNCH
IZZZT
ZZZZT
IF I'M GOING TO HAVE ANY CHANCE WITH THIS GUY, I 'M GOING TO HAVE TO MOVE THIS FIGHT TO A LESS WOODED AREA.
YOU NEED TO LEARN QUICKLY, RED ONE!
YOU CANNOT DEFEAT ME! I WILL BE RULER HERE AS I HAVE BEEN IN THE PAST!

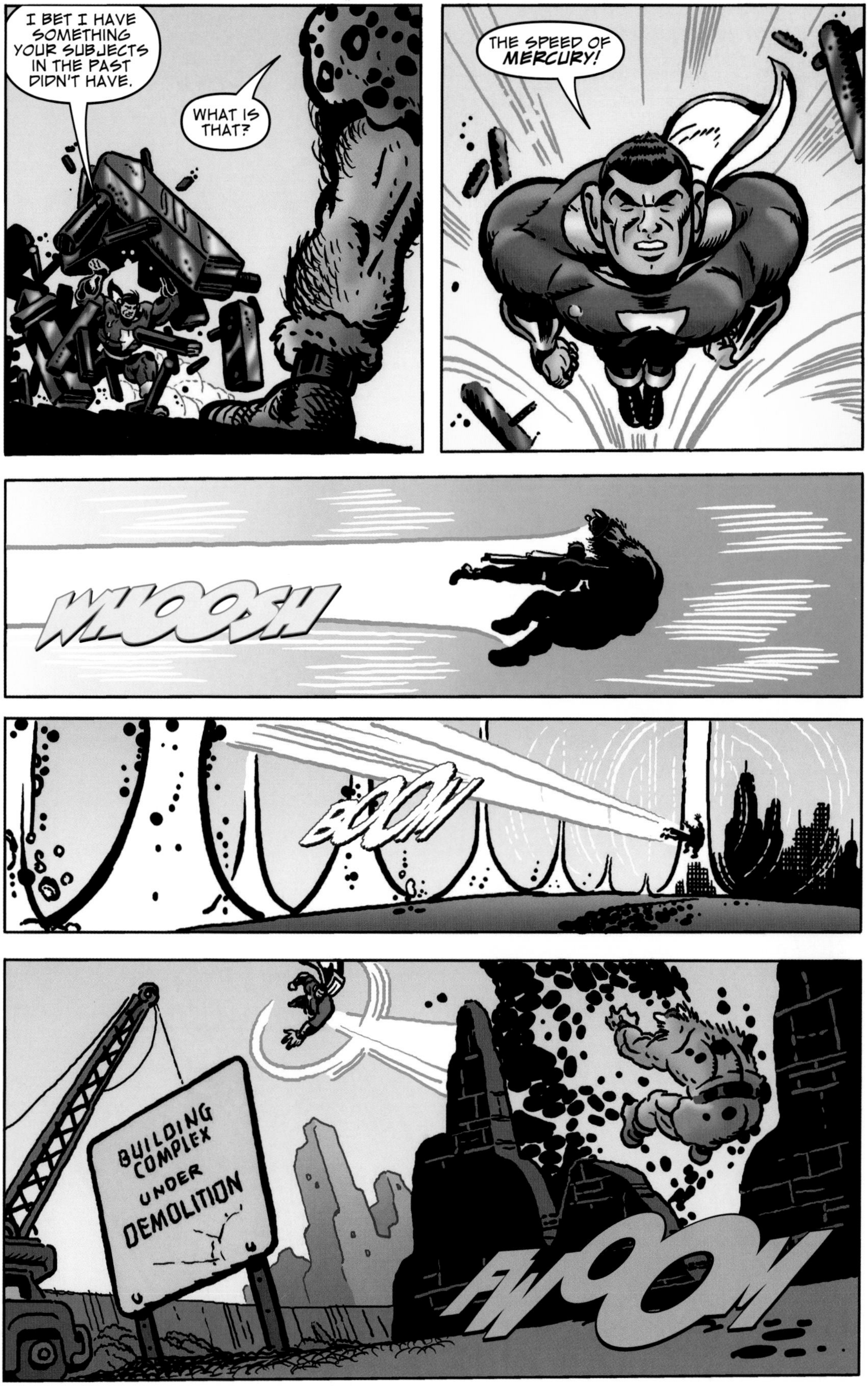
I BET I HAVE SOMETHING YOUR SUBJECTS IN THE PAST DIDN'T HAVE.
WHAT IS THAT?
THE SPEED OF MERCURY!
WHOOSH
BOOM
BUILDING COMPLEX UNDER DEMOLITION
FWOOOM

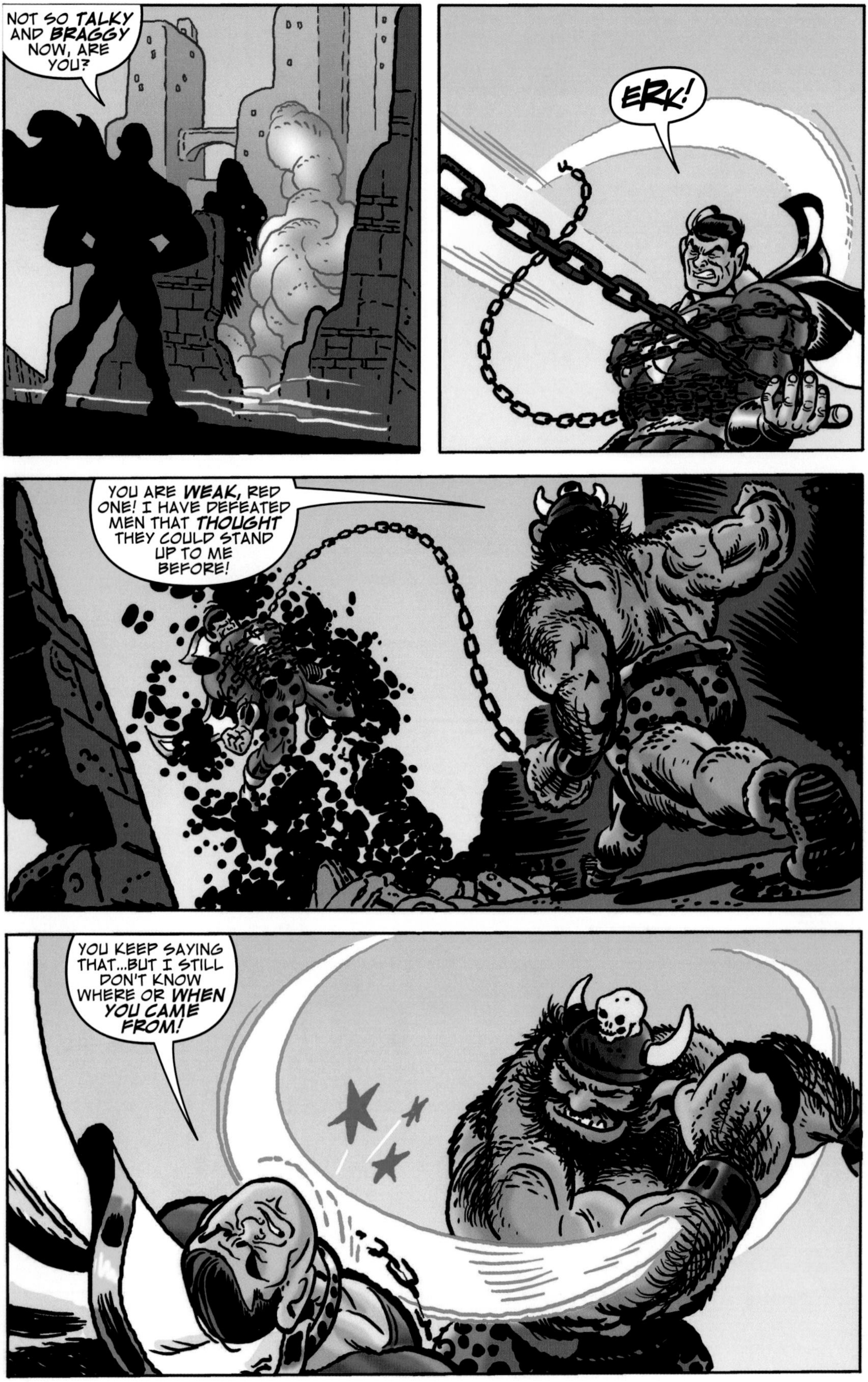
NOT SO TALKY AND BRAGGY NOW, ARE YOU?
ERK!
YOU ARE WEAK, RED ONE! I HAVE DEFEATED MEN THAT THOUGHT THEY COULD STAND UP TO ME BEFORE!
YOU KEEP SAYING THAT...BUT I STILL DON'T KNOW WHERE OR WHEN YOU CAME FROM!

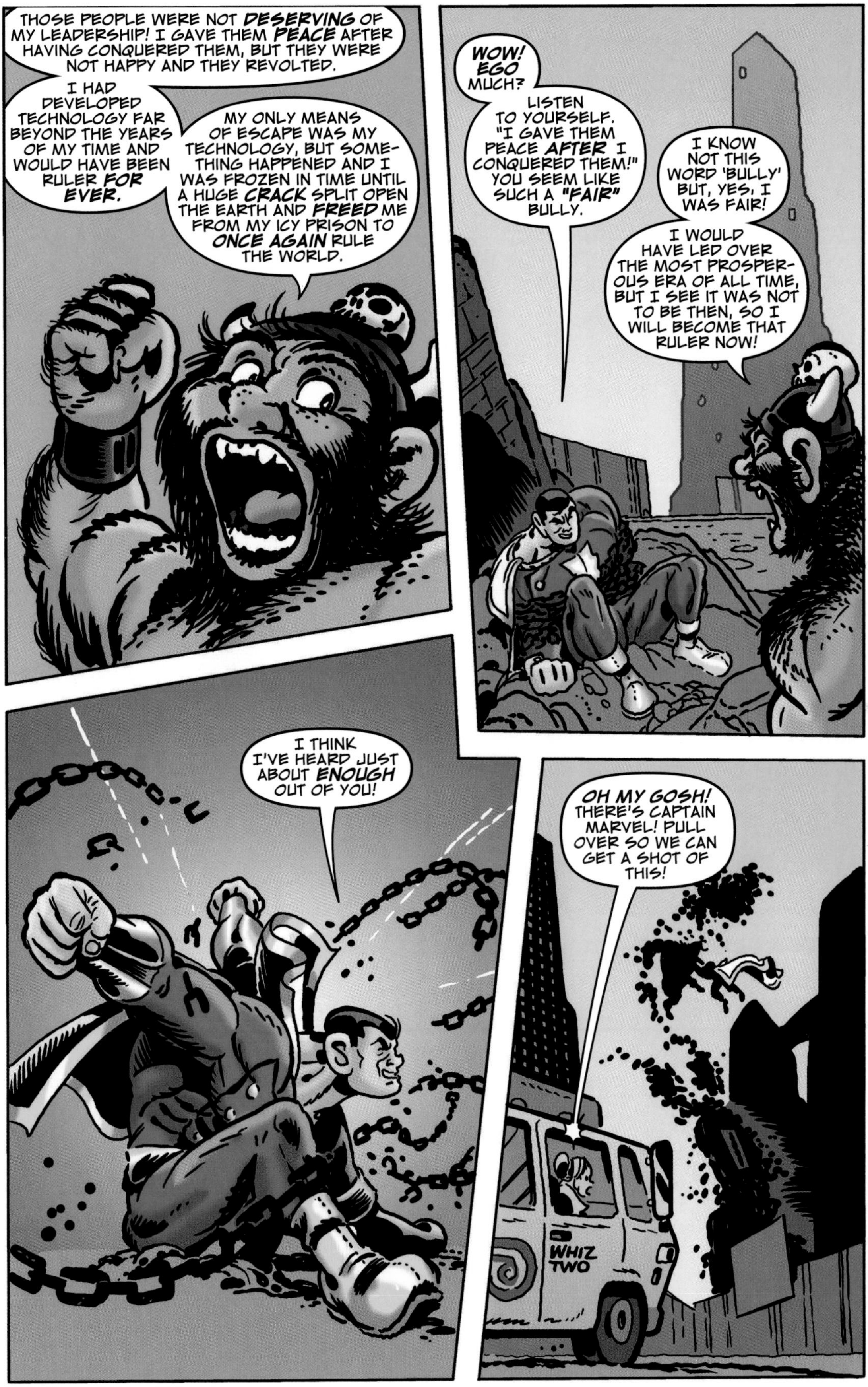
THOSE PEOPLE WERE NOT DESERVING OF MY LEADERSHIP! I GAVE THEM PEACE AFTER HAVING CONQUERED THEM, BUT THEY WERE NOT HAPPY AND THEY REVOLTED.
I HAD DEVELOPED TECHNOLOGY FAR BEYOND THE YEARS OF MY TIME AND WOULD HAVE BEEN RULER FOR EVER.
MY ONLY MEANS OF ESCAPE WAS MY TECHNOLOGY, BUT SOME-THING HAPPENED AND I WAS FROZEN IN TIME UNTIL A HUGE CRACK SPLIT OPEN THE EARTH AND FREED ME FROM MY ICY PRISON TO ONCE AGAIN RULE THE WORLD.
WOW! EGO MUCH?
LISTEN TO YOURSELF. "I GAVE THEM PEACE AFTER I CONQUERED THEM!" YOU SEEM LIKE SUCH A "FAIR" BULLY.
I KNOW NOT THIS WORD 'BULLY' BUT, YES, I WAS FAIR!
I WOULD HAVE LED OVER THE MOST PROSPER-OUS ERA OF ALL TIME, BUT I SEE IT WAS NOT TO BE THEN, SO I WILL BECOME THAT RULER NOW!
I THINK I'VE HEARD JUST ABOUT ENOUGH OUT OF YOU!
OH MY GOSH! THERE'S CAPTAIN MARVEL! PULL OVER SO WE CAN GET A SHOT OF THIS!
WHIZ TWO

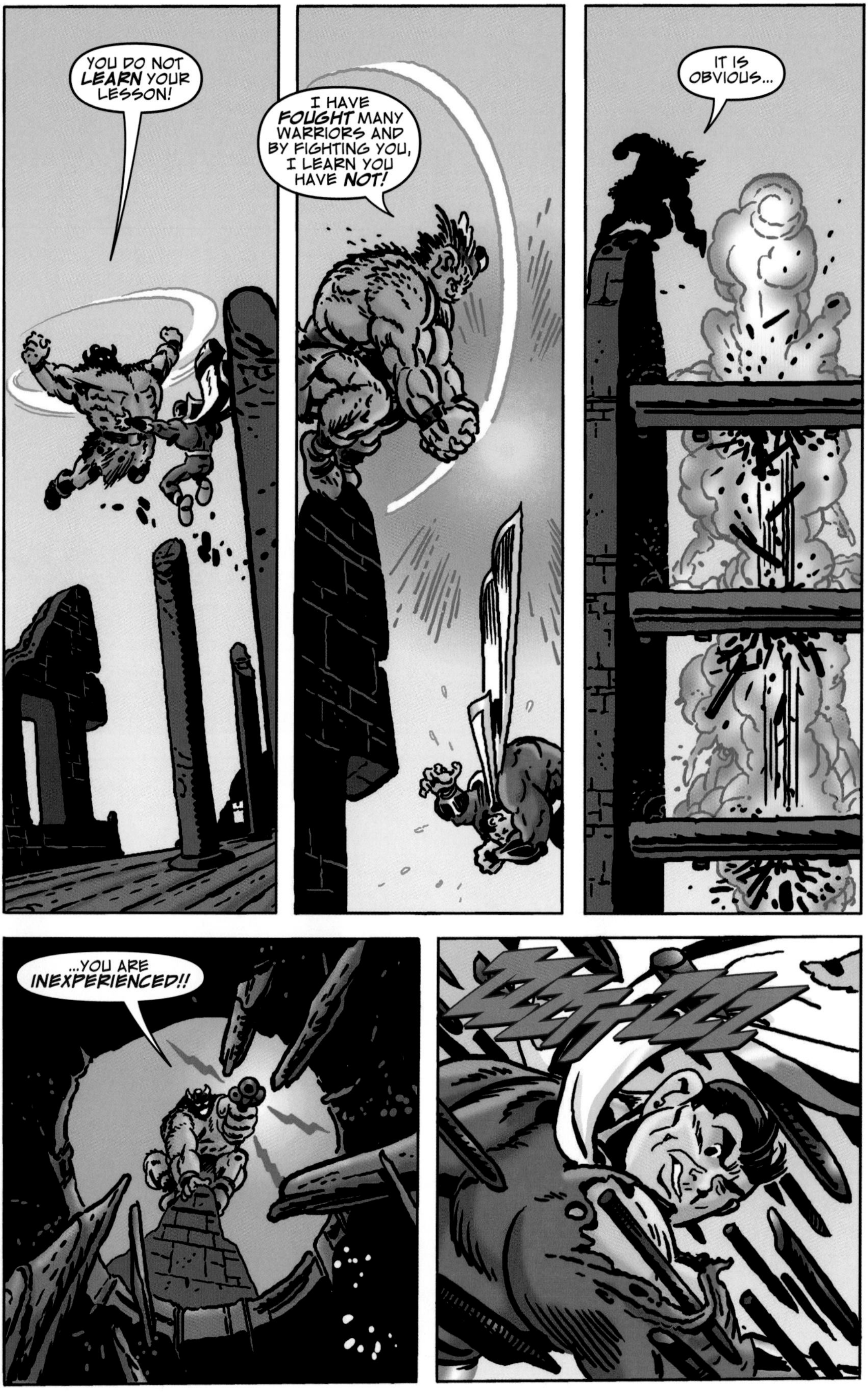
YOU DO NOT LEARN YOUR LESSON!
I HAVE FOUGHT MANY WARRIORS AND BY FIGHTING YOU, I LEARN YOU HAVE NOT!
IT IS OBVIOUS...
...YOU ARE INEXPERIENCED!!

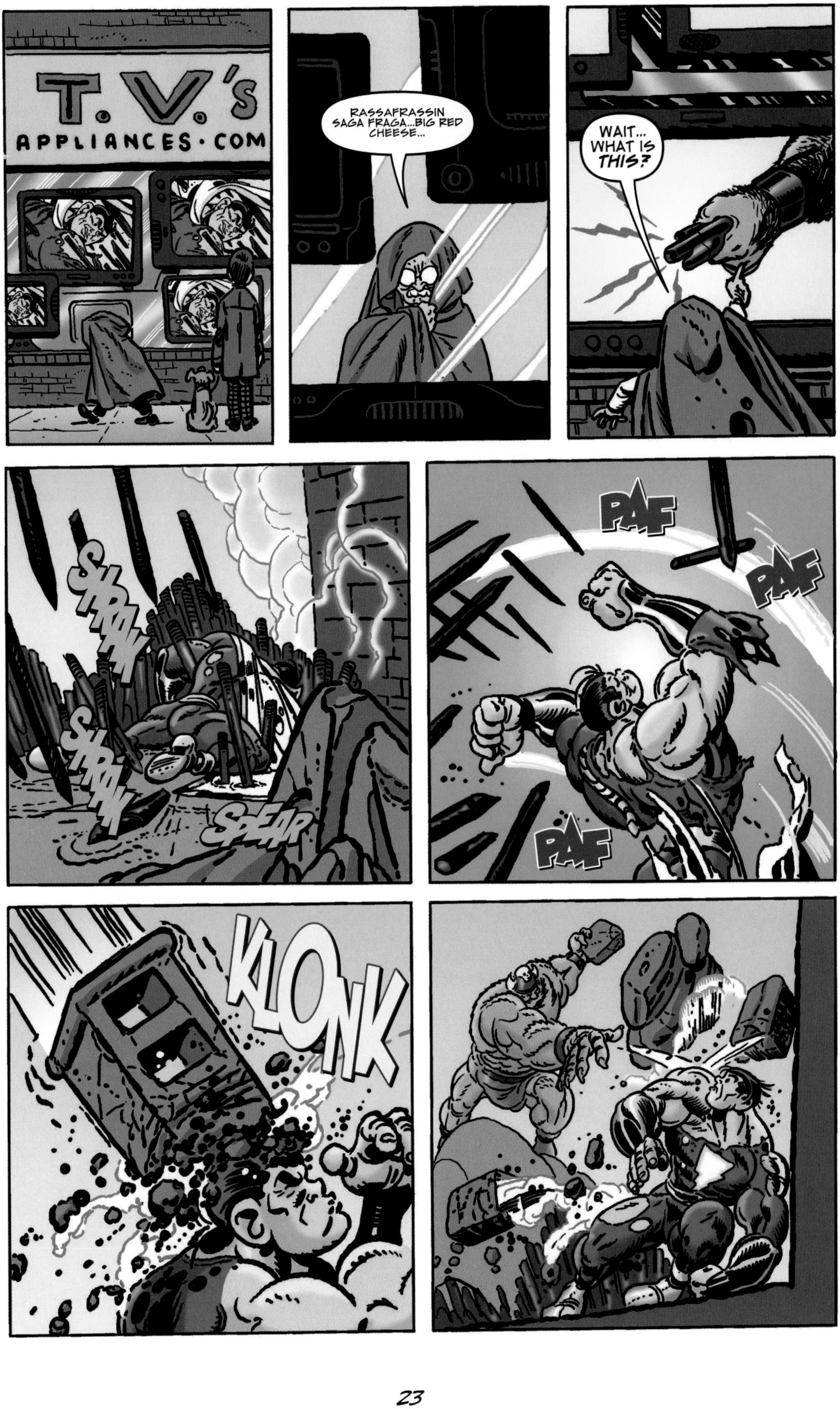
T.V.'s
APPLIANCES·COM
RASSAFRASSIN SAGA FRAGA...BIG RED CHEESE...
WAIT... WHAT IS THIS?
SHRAK
SHRAK
SPEAR
PAF
PAF
PAF
KLONK

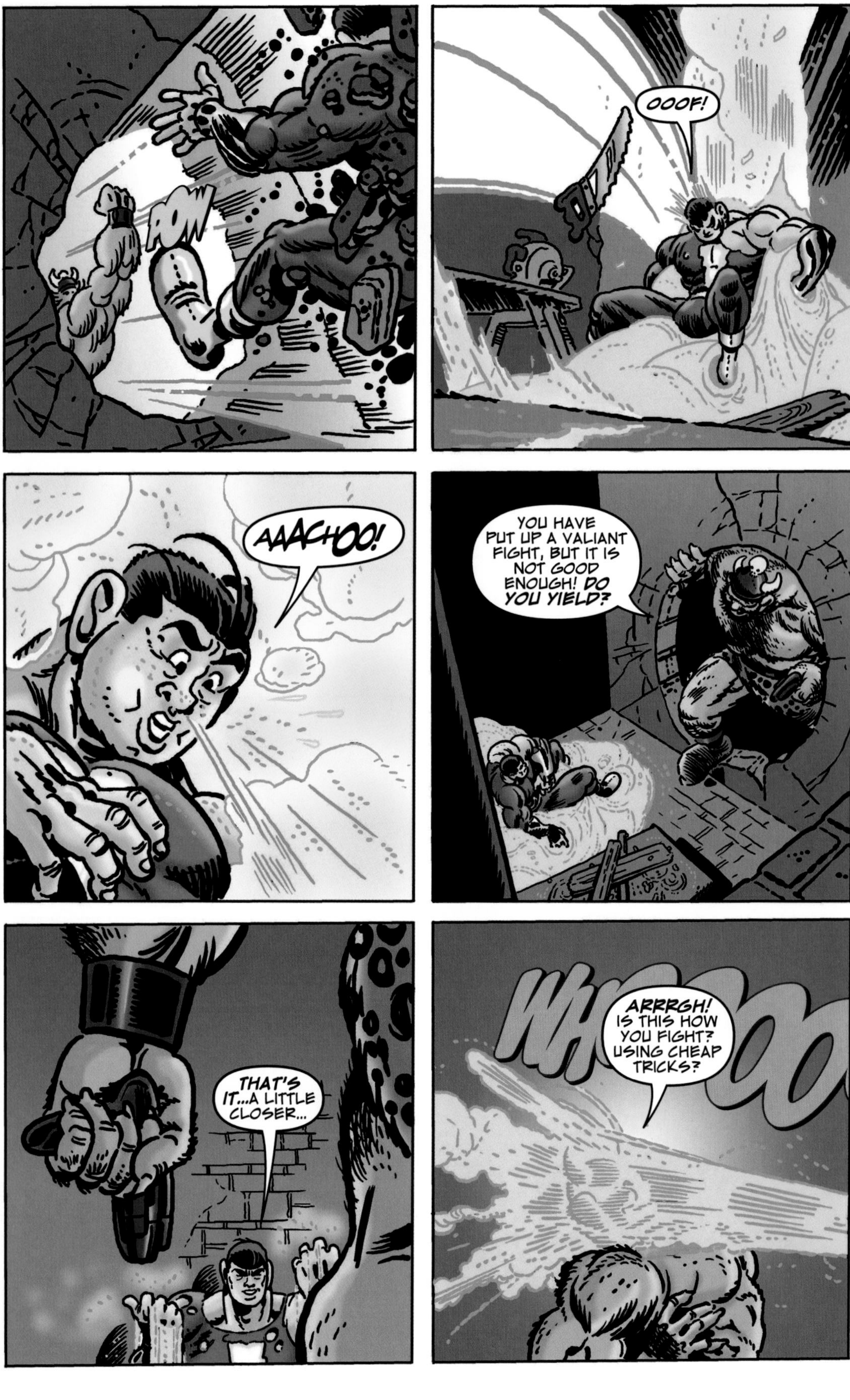
POW
OOOF!
AAACHOO!
YOU HAVE PUT UP A VALIANT FIGHT, BUT IT IS NOT GOOD ENOUGH! DO YOU YIELD?
THAT'S IT...A LITTLE CLOSER...
ARRRGH! IS THIS HOW YOU FIGHT? USING CHEAP TRICKS?

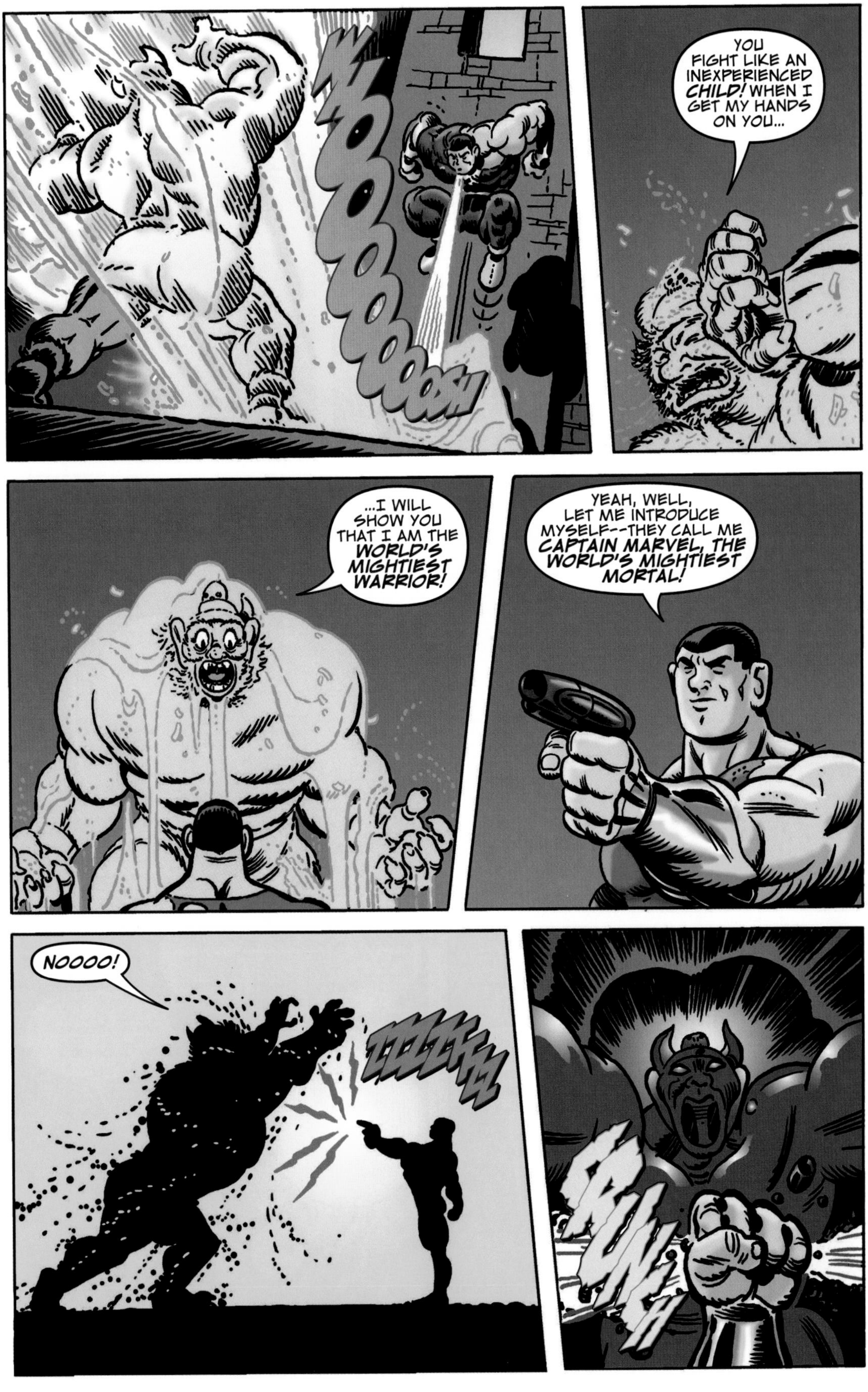
WHOOOOOOOOOSH
YOU FIGHT LIKE AN INEXPERIENCED CHILD! WHEN I GET MY HANDS ON YOU...
...I WILL SHOW YOU THAT I AM THE WORLD'S MIGHTIEST WARRIOR!
YEAH, WELL, LET ME INTRODUCE MYSELF--THEY CALL ME CAPTAIN MARVEL, THE WORLD'S MIGHTIEST MORTAL!
NOOOO!
ZZZZKKK
PUNCH

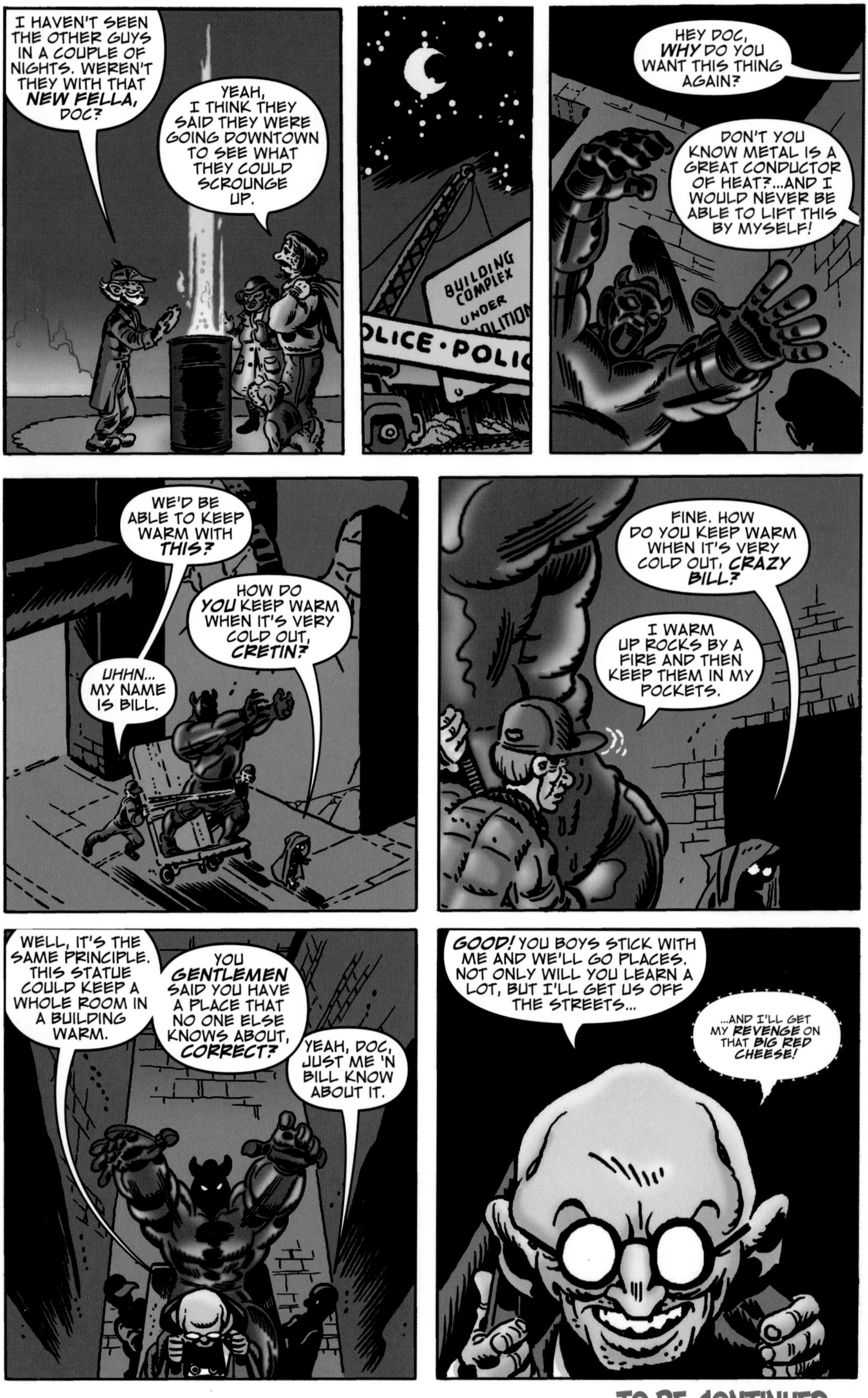
I HAVEN'T SEEN THE OTHER GUYS IN A COUPLE OF NIGHTS. WEREN'T THEY WITH THAT NEW FELLA, DOC?
YEAH, I THINK THEY SAID THEY WERE GOING DOWNTOWN TO SEE WHAT THEY COULD SCROUNGE UP.
BUILDING COMPLEX UNDER ...OLITION
...LICE · POLIC...
HEY DOC, WHY DO YOU WANT THIS THING AGAIN?
DON'T YOU KNOW METAL IS A GREAT CONDUCTOR OF HEAT?...AND I WOULD NEVER BE ABLE TO LIFT THIS BY MYSELF!
WE'D BE ABLE TO KEEP WARM WITH THIS?
HOW DO YOU KEEP WARM WHEN IT'S VERY COLD OUT, CRETIN?
UHHN... MY NAME IS BILL.
FINE. HOW DO YOU KEEP WARM WHEN IT'S VERY COLD OUT, CRAZY BILL?
I WARM UP ROCKS BY A FIRE AND THEN KEEP THEM IN MY POCKETS.
WELL, IT'S THE SAME PRINCIPLE. THIS STATUE COULD KEEP A WHOLE ROOM IN A BUILDING WARM.
YOU GENTLEMEN SAID YOU HAVE A PLACE THAT NO ONE ELSE KNOWS ABOUT, CORRECT?
YEAH, DOC, JUST ME 'N BILL KNOW ABOUT IT.
GOOD! YOU BOYS STICK WITH ME AND WE'LL GO PLACES. NOT ONLY WILL YOU LEARN A LOT, BUT I'LL GET US OFF THE STREETS...
...AND I'LL GET MY REVENGE ON THAT BIG RED CHEESE!

TO BE CONTINUED...

CREATORS

ART BALTAZAR – CO-WRITER

Born in Chicago, **Art Baltazar** has been cartooning ever since he can recall. Art has worked on award-winning series like Tiny Titans and Superman Family Adventures. He lives outside of Chicago with his wife, Rose, and children Sonny, Gordon, and Audrey.

FRANCO – CO-WRITER

Franco Aureliani has been drawing comics ever since he could hold a crayon. He resides in upstate New York with his wife, Ivette, and son, Nicolas, and spends most of his days working on comics. Franco has worked on Superman Family Adventures and Tiny Titans, and he also teaches high school art.

GLOSSARY

brutish (BROO-tish)--cruel, violent, stupid, or beast-like

complacent (kuhm-PLAY-suhnt)--satisfied with how things are and not wanting to change them

conductor (kuhn-DUCK-tohr)--a person who stands in front of people while they sing or play musical instruments and directs their performance, or a person who collects money or tickets from passengers on a train

conquer (KONG-ker)--to defeat something or someone by the use of force

ditch (DITCH)--abandon

eternity (i-TER-ni-tee)--time without an end

hoax (HOHKS)--an act that is meant to trick or deceive people

obvious (AHB-vee-uhss)--easy for the mind to see, understand, or recognize

penitentiary (pen-i-TEN-shuh-ree)--prison

priority (pry-OR-uh-tee)--something that is more important than other things and that needs to be done or dealt with first

puny (PYOO-nee)--small and weak

slight (SLAHYT)--very small in degree or amount

voodoo (VOO-doo)--a religion that is practiced chiefly in Haiti and is often associated with magic and spells

VISUAL QUESTIONS & PROMPTS

1. What is this thing that King Kull uses? What does it do? How do you know?

2. Billy beat King Kull by using his own weapon against him. What are some other ways King Kull could've been defeated by Billy?

3. Why is Dr. Sivana's speech bubble dashed? Why is the text smaller? Explain your answer.

GOOD! YOU BOYS STICK WITH ME AND WE'LL GO PLACES. NOT ONLY WILL YOU LEARN A LOT, BUT I'LL GET US OFF THE STREETS...
...AND I'LL GET MY REVENGE ON THAT BIG RED CHEESE!
3

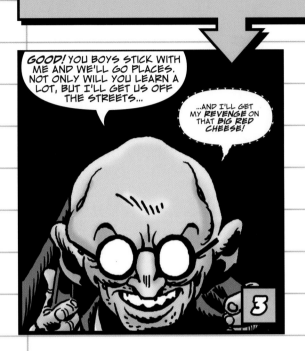

4. What are some other ways King Kull could have used his weapon to fight Billy Batson?

4

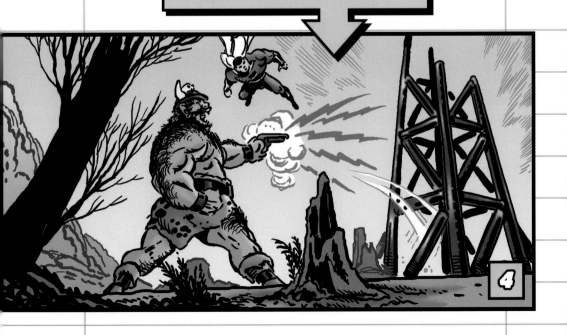

READ THEM ALL!

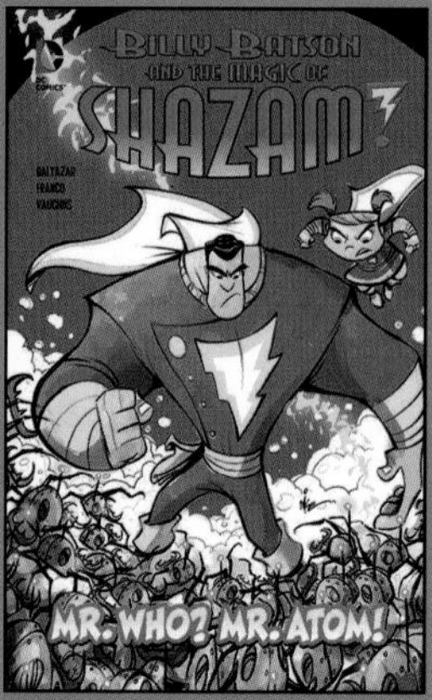
BILLY BATSON AND THE MAGIC OF SHAZAM!
BALTAZAR
FRANCO
VAUGHNS
MR. WHO? MR. ATOM!

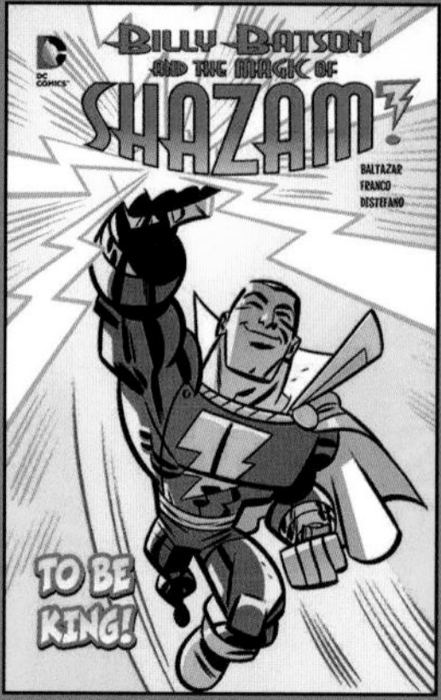
BILLY BATSON AND THE MAGIC OF SHAZAM!
BALTAZAR
FRANCO
DESTEFANO
TO BE KING!

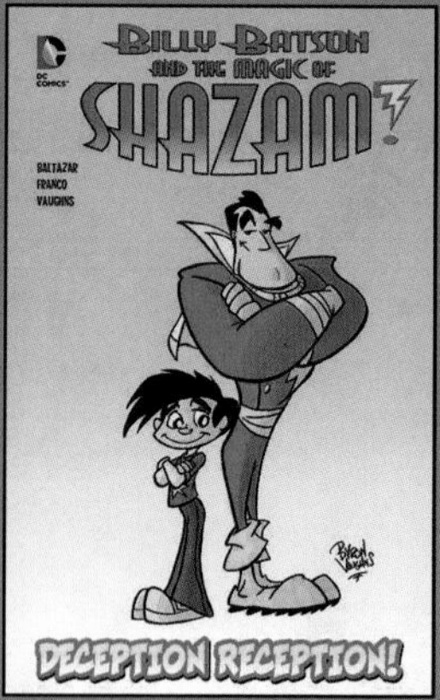
BILLY BATSON AND THE MAGIC OF SHAZAM!
BALTAZAR
FRANCO
VAUGHNS
DECEPTION RECEPTION!

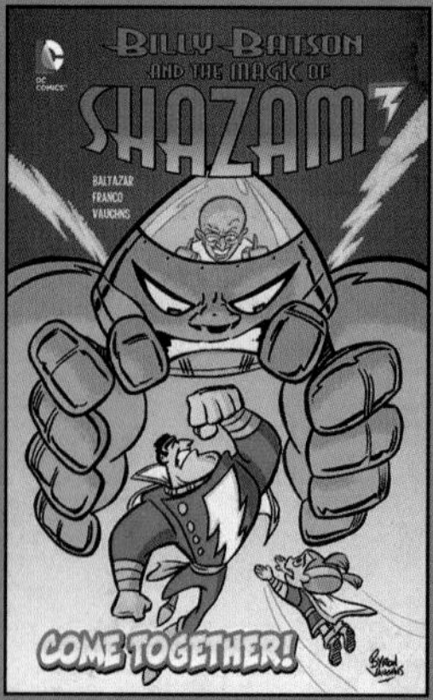
BILLY BATSON AND THE MAGIC OF SHAZAM!
BALTAZAR
FRANCO
VAUGHNS
COME TOGETHER!

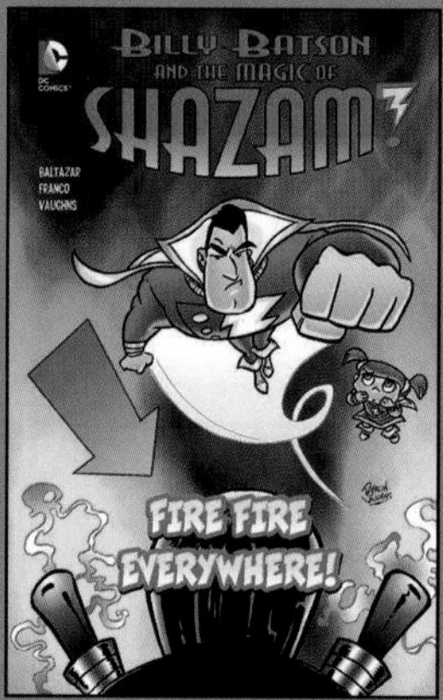
BILLY BATSON AND THE MAGIC OF SHAZAM!
BALTAZAR
FRANCO
VAUGHNS
FIRE FIRE EVERYWHERE!

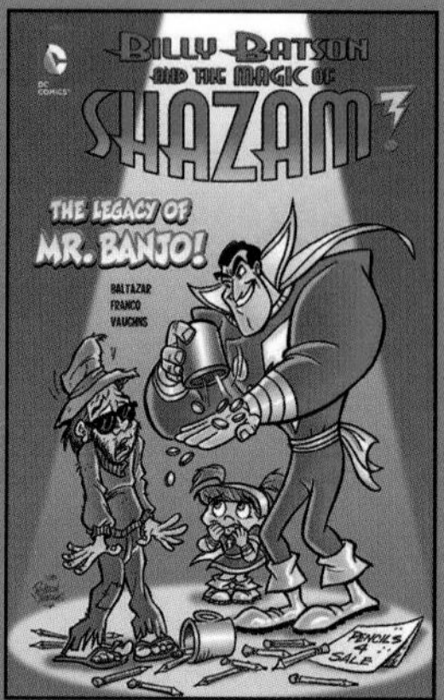
BILLY BATSON AND THE MAGIC OF SHAZAM!
THE LEGACY OF MR. BANJO!
BALTAZAR
FRANCO
VAUGHNS
PENCILS 4 SALE

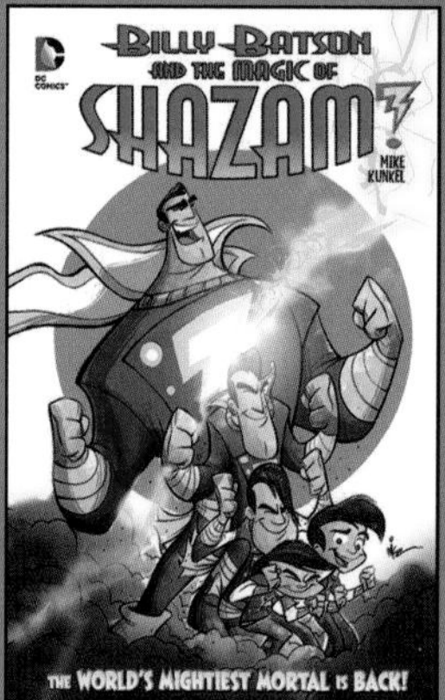
BILLY BATSON AND THE MAGIC OF SHAZAM!
MIKE KUNKEL
THE WORLD'S MIGHTIEST MORTAL IS BACK!

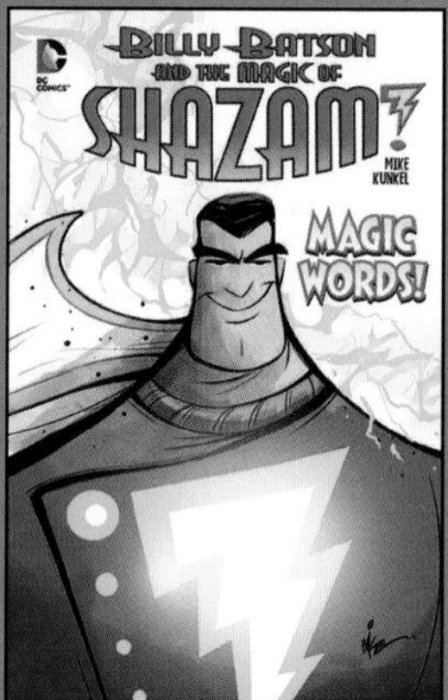
BILLY BATSON AND THE MAGIC OF SHAZAM!
MIKE KUNKEL
MAGIC WORDS!

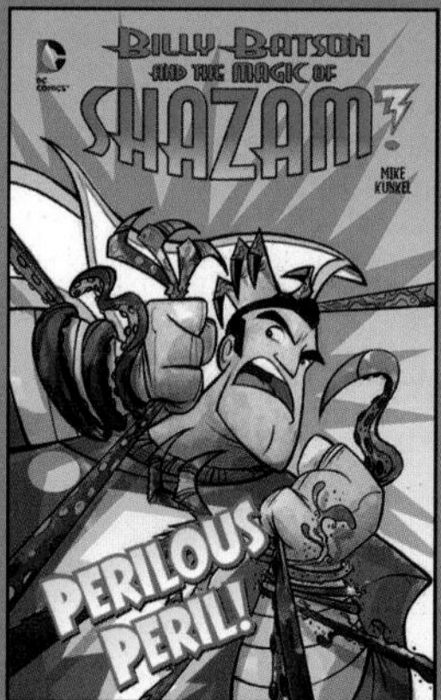
BILLY BATSON AND THE MAGIC OF SHAZAM!
MIKE KUNKEL
PERILOUS PERIL!

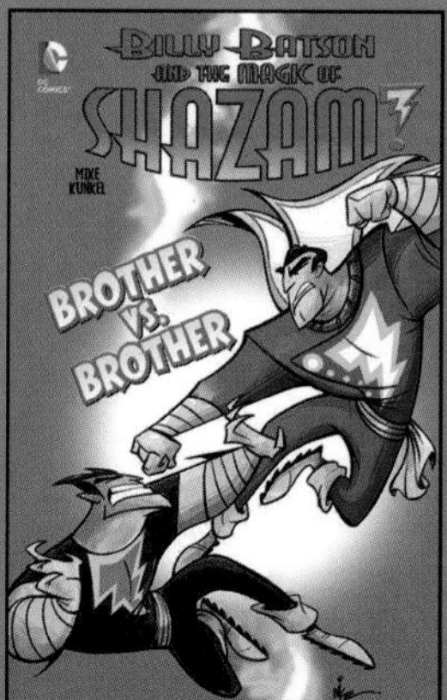
BILLY BATSON AND THE MAGIC OF SHAZAM!
MIKE KUNKEL
BROTHER VS. BROTHER